WORDS UNSPOKEN

FANATIXX PUBLICATION
ISO 9001:2015 CERTIFIED

FanatiXx Publication
AM/56, Basanti Colony, Rourkela 769012, Odisha
ISO 9001:2015 CERTIFIED
Website: www.fanatixx.in

© Copyright, 2019, Amoolya Tripathi

" Words Unspoken "

By: Amoolya Tripathi

ISBN: 978-93-89106-21-3

Hindi Poetry Anthology 1st Edition

Book Formatting: Saizal Gupta | **Cover Design:** Hemant Bansal

The opinions/contents expressed in this book are solely of the author and do not represent the opinions/ standings/ thoughts of FanatiXx.

<u>CO-AUTHORS</u>

1. **Pari Raheja**
2. **Shubhi Awasthi**
3. **Abhishek Yadav**
4. **Suchismita Ghoshal**
5. **Rahul Pasumarthy**
6. **Ritobrata Das**
7. **Samriddhi Gupta**
8. **Upen Reddy**
9. **Subhashini Natarajan**
10. **Sharayu Salunkhe**
11. **Neha Mandal-**
12. **Rashmitha Kapuganti**
13. **Srashti Srivastava**
14. **Aarti Shahdadpuri**
15. **Dev Jhawar**
16. **Sneha Tiwari**
17. **Manali Debroy**
18. **Naman Srivastava**
19. **Himanshi**
20. **Nimmi**
21. **Anisha Chakraborty**
22. **Harish Labana**
23. **Khushi Bano Nadri**

24. **Anjali Chandak**
25. **Akshita Agarwal**
26. **Mahak Sharma**
27. **Vedika Beriwal**
28. **Manshi Toshniwal**
29. **Sauhard Pandey**
30. **Mansavi Parmar**
31. **Rashmitha Kapuganti**

Amoolya Tripathi

(Founder ALFAAZ)

FOUNDER'S MESSAGE

It all began with a thought…

It seemed incredible and out of reach when I started to achieve something there are several thought in my mind that I should give up but you know as they say work until achieve success and thinking thus, I started with this book "WORDS UNSPOKEN". Where I wanted to give the budding writers a chance to showcase their talents, I am proud to present to you WORDS UNSPOKEN 31 Feelings and 31 Jazbaat.

 This anthology has been a journey of hard work, hours of continuous editing and chaos that arose almost daily. but with the patience of my team and their trust in me, we move ahead. Thank you to all those who were a part of this journey. and apologies to those whom I caused inconvenience. above all, my deepest gratitude to my parents and Shoeb Ali who supported me throughout. without Mahadev's blessings this book has been in complete.

-Amoolya Tripathi

Founder ALFAAZ

Pari Raheja

She is a student of class 11th and loves to write. Her hobbies are singing and dancing. She is a p.c.m student- "Loves to live life to the fullest."

She

She is a daughter, Free to enjoy laughter. She is a girl,

Born to desire. She is a lady, wishing to aspire. She is a

female,

wanting to be stronger than a male.

She is a wife,

Always ready to strive.

She is a mother,

Who binds a family together? She is a WOMAN,

Not less than the Wonder Woman.

There comes

There comes the cloud's, With their wool like body.
Finding their way through the crowd, for this is their hobby.

There comes the sun, with all its gaiety.
For all the darkness to shun, in such a great variety.

There comes the rain,
To take away all the pain.

There come the birds, With their light feathers.
To play their vocal cords, and overwhelm others.

There comes the Nature, to heal all the wounds.
And all the lovely creatures, to give us great fortunes.

Life: A sea of difficulties

How was the exam? Her mother asked.
'Despondent', her face blanched.

What happened? Mother was alarmed. Nothing but the
exam was hard.
Don't be sad, the mother consoled. Crying and crying, her
face was pale.
It's just another exam tale.

Life is tough, learn to be happy,

But the small girl was gripped with agony. The mother
served her favorite dish, but there was no sign of bliss.
Every day is a challenge, Accept it.

Don't be afraid, strongly face it.

Hard work and passion never go in vain, Now please come
out of your pain.
The girl was mirthful, feeling calm, Determined and
motivated,
She clapped her palm.

मेरा भारत महान

जहाँ एक त्योहार को मान्यता देता,
आज यह सारा संसार है ।
वही हर त्योहार की ख़ुशियाँ देता,
मेरा भारत महान है ।

जहाँ हर डाली ,हर बेल में,
खिलखिलाती हुई मुस्कान है।
ऐसा ही एक दृश्य देता,
मेरा भारत महान है।

गंगा जमुना सरस्वती संगम की शान है,
जहाँ बारह वर्ष में सजता कुम्भ का महा स्नान है ।
इठलाती झलमल बहती झेलम और चेनब है,
शीश उठाए मुकुट सजाए हिम पर्वत तो ढाल है ।

ऐसे देश की बोलो बंधु
और कोई मिसाल है,
हा जी हा
यह मेरा भारत महान है !

Shubhi Awasthi

She is a student who is pursuing Humanities. She was not very much interested in writing but got influenced by her best friend who is a writer. She is a very cheerful and a talkative person.

बचपन की यादें कहां गई वो रातें जब मां मुझे लोरियां सुनाया करती थी, कहां गए वो पल जब पापा मेरे लिए चॉक्लेट लाया करते थे। कहां गई वो शाम जब बाबा मुझे घुमाने ले जाया करते , कहां गए वो लम्हें जब दादी मुझे कहानियां सुनाया करती थीं। कहां गया वो समय जब भाई से छोटी-छोटी चीजों के लिए लड़ा करती थी, और मिल जाने फूलें न समाती। कहां गई वो लड़ाईयां जब दीदी हमेशा मेरे साथ होती थी । कहां गए वो दिन जब दोस्तों के साथ घर-घर खेला करती थी। कहां गई वो खुशियां जो साथ में मिलकर मनाया करते थे।

THE PERFECT BEST FRIEND

An angel perhaps you could quite easily be, Reflecting
heavenly warmth surely special to see,
You must have been sent only for me from the heaven
above, because you're always radiating divine care and
love.

When I feel absolutely low and depressed,
I can feel your concern, the depth of which no one can
comprehend. True friendship is a blessing rare,
Yet in my life, I looked up at you and you were there.

Finding a friend that is so special and true, isn't that
easy and I'm really lucky to have you,
The world, indeed wears a smile on his face, when
people like you make it such a nicer place.

Abhishek Yadav

Hey, I'm Abhishek. I entered in this world when I was living with Loneliness. Now it's my Best Hobby. I'm Pursuing B.Tech.

Rain

The rain on some day's whispers to me,

'Hey',

Just come with me under the open sky.

Open your arms, I'll fill you with emotive emotions.

Come down on the ground and enjoy the scent of wet soil.

Come on, Let the drops of rain come

to your face, and enjoy its sound.

Come on, Color yourself with every single drop of rain.

Come on, open the window and put your head on pillow

and close your eyes, feel the wind on your face.

You can make this moment special by 'Hot coffee'.

Suchismita Ghoshal

Hey, this is Suchismita Ghoshal from West Bengal, India. Her schooling was completed from Barlow Girls High School in Malda in 2016. She is 21 & pursuing her graduation in Zoology in Malda College. She has always been a curious soul from childhood & used to observe things intensely. She belongs from a small town but her dreams are to touch the sky keeping her feet to the ground. She loves to read ponderous amount of books & this left an impact on writing by her own. She has been in this profession for 4 years & loves to write poetry, short story & anything inspires her. She enhances her writing skill by feeling each & every incident through her heart. She loves travelling and gaining knowledge's beside writing. She aspires to be a good writer as well as a book reviewer in near future.

BIRTHDAY WISH

The clock hits 12' again, Eyes wide open enough,
yet feels like waking up from a dream; The hues of green,
blue, yellow & red, disperse from the core of my heart.
The series of wishes catches my breath, still my ears yearn for
the sweetest one, Unheard & unmatched;
Restless shadows sketch my lingers,
I feel the shivers from my head to toe. the moon away from
million miles, greets with its silver tints;
I watch the glee of glistening stars, hailing for a new start!
My fingers caress my strands of hair, the thought restricts
on a pending wish, my nails scratch the window panes,
the desires latch on an unfulfilled message. It pains where
three words are tougher to get,
It dries throat if easiest things are rarest to touch,
It wets eyes when attuned gazes turn into unseen thirsts
Among the delicate chocolates & candies,
I wait for the embrace interlocking my broken pieces, I long
for the forehead-kiss curing my wounds,
I crave for the lap enriching my peace-world. It shows 5
minutes past to 12,
waking up from a fake reverie,
I knew it won't come again,
the new start won't be ravishing again,
the radiant hues won't show his path again,
the presents won't unfasten the lost memories again;
My birthday will come & go,
Aging will make my experiences grow;
But all I know they can't cover,
Can never cover my longing for my dad again.

Shattered or, Recovered?

After so many days, I looked down, I looked down to the soil of this ground. After so many days, I felt a way out of being imprisoned. I knew I had seen a lot. I had told a lot. I had gone through a lot. Now, I just wanted one drop of serene showered in my mind. I wished if the wind could be a little more hushed and soothing to feel it with all my being. I wanted nothing more than an antidote of peace. Last time when I came here, one year ago, I laughed with her, I saw her acting like a child and I couldn't even keep my eyes away from her for a second. She was an aroma never to be forgotten, an eden never to be lost and a consolation never to be unaccepted. I used to feel warm whenever she electrified with her one touch & her smile used to heal my pains. Anyway, I am now busy searching our footprints here, perhaps long thrusted along with numerous footprints.

Huh...I took a long sigh!

Alleys of my memories are now embedded with a small drop of aches in each one. I wanted to scream loudly & tell everyone how I have been without her. But, I didn't. I lost her the day we fought in our trust issues. She bided me the last goodbye swiping off her tears & I just remained as a silent witness with heart-aches. Trust me, I cried. I cried a lot & spent speechless nights. Her absence tormented me and haunted me like hell. I couldn't rescue myself. I counted stars in my insomnia & always thought whether she felt just like me or not! Then one fine day, I watched with another guy smilingly taking selfies while passing this ground. Perhaps, she didn't notice me. I couldn't utter any words & noticed that my cheeks were wet with two or three drops of my tears. I swiped off them. I barely had control over myself but I had to. I wasn't bereaved that she replaced me easily, but I was upset that our promises had no values! I won't say I don't love her. Still I love her, but now I am isolated with the fact of love. I hate the fact of cupped palms & fake determination of staying together. Nothing lasts forever. Believe or not, if something lasts, that your memories which you take in your funeral with yourself. This 'memory' lasts forever. Yes, today I looked down, looked down to see the ring she gifted me still shining in my finger. I looked down to gather my shattered pieces. Looked down to collect my ability to be recovered.

Rahul Pasumarthy

Rahul Pasumarthy is 20 years old, a boy from Vizianagaram. he is a CA student a part from his studies, he wrote stories and motivational quotes, he was a moody writer and bookaholic. His dream was to inspire millions of people in following their dreams and motivate them to face their failure and believe and fall in love, he wrote about life, love, pain, healing and recovery.

Phone ringing.

Hello! This is Arnav.

Hello, bhai, our results are out just now, go and check your marks. Finally, after three continuous failures. Now I'm a CA final student.
You passed. Abhijith?

Yes!!! I qualified. And I hope you will too.

After ending the call, I opened the website icai org. In this is some mini heart stroke while opening it. And the rest is hell. These is 5 time I failed again.
Suddenly eyes were surrounded by the tears. Heart increased his weight. Brain started sending negative thoughts. And I broke out, cried loud. What the fuck is happening in my life? After every failure, I started preparation to giving my best. And improving myself to be a right one to qualify. However, nothing is changed in my result card. I think me and a pregnancy woman only the value of nine months. In these nine months. I get criticisms, heart breaks, negative thoughts, tears, pain, stress, depression what not all the things have entered into my life. That day when the whole world left me those things entered into my life. I recollected my nine months' time in few seconds and I took the phone to call mom and say about my result.
Hello mom!
Aranav say, this is dad.
This is the thing which I don't want to be happen, but I don't know why god is too harsh to me...

Hello dad, how are you,

Yeah, I'm fine. I think results are out right, what happen to yours?

Dad, I failed.

You failed! Are you serious? This is the 5th time, I already said to you at the beginning that you are unfit for CA and with your over confidence you said I will do. And now are struck ed in a think layered mud. in which you can't go to the end or even come back. With your foolishness, you put yourself in those type of miserable situations. You are an idiot, if you are not interested than say. You are just wasting money and time. I and mom are feeling guilty to talk about you. How can we talk on behalf of a child who is incapable of clearing one examination from past two years? Go to hell aranav. I can't help you in this situation. If you want any money ask your mom.
Bye.

Even though those words are not common to me. After hearing them in my dad's voice made me a little low. All the people are seeing my failures. However, no one is seeing my hard work, pain and the situation I'm undergone. This society is designed to depress you. I'm living in a family in which parents feel proud to talk about their children qualification rather than their personal topics.
The thing is all courses are not designed equally. This truth is hidden in the darkness of the society. While everyone is running towards engineering, there are few people like me who challenged their life my opting a non-engineering course. This is not the pain of mine this is the common emotion of every student who wanted to challenge their lives by choosing different career.

I think if we start practicing the suggestion which we give to others, then we will be in a high position. We are living in a society where people have a no money to give you, but people have so many suggestions to confuse you. Change doesn't come in a night in the life of a family. I took a stand to do different and change the life of my family at least for the future generations.

I'm the person who does pgbp (profit or gain from business or profession) rather than pubg. I'm the person who uses a calculator more than phone. I'm the person who is in a living relationship with my books. However, I don't know why the result is not changed.

In those two years, I learned a lot of things how to live solely, struggle solely, fight independently, the difference between expectations and hope. Because when you opted a different path then you must be prepared that you have to travel solely. Nobody is there to console, motivate, travel with you. I had many heart breaks during these two years, but at the end I realized that I am the only one with myself and what may be the situations. I had only two people with me in my life, they are mom and dad. These all stuff are common to me. I decided to start my preparation for my next attempt. I decided to join in the coaching center to feel better. This is all for this day.

Good night.

Morning 9:30.

Oh! God. This is my first day to college, and I'm late. I rushed to class. It is already started. I said my apologies and entered into the class. It's almost full. I felt a little hard to find a place to sit. At lost I have seen a chair beside a girl, and then I make my way to that chair. After sitting the chair. My heart is pinching me to see the girls face. However, I'm somewhat introvert, I have just seen his high heels and then his hair. His hair is smells like a perfume. And finally, I have seen her face. Oh! Shit man, this is the girl who broken my heart earlier. It is such a pain full thing this world. Then she looked at me, and I have just given a weird smile and ran away from the class. I decided to not to attend the class. I just started preparing my exams from sitting in my room. Finally, I have done with my exams, and results are out. I think that I did my best. However, god has planned something different than I thought.

And I failed in this attempt too. Even so, this time is somewhat different. And I got a call from the girl who left me and said she qualified and said thanks for not attending the class. So, because of your absence, I concentrated more and qualified. Then I literally understood how fool I'm. Because of her I didn't attend the class. However, she hurt me more. Then to share my grief, I called to my mom. She started scolding me and she said one thing, which hurt me. You are just born to degrade our prestige. If I knew you are such a person. I wish I could not give birth to you.

These words let me to take a decision. SUICIDE.

Many people like me. Who want to change their family position, for better life? However, they are left as an isolated one. Every night I cry, cry for something I want badly, but I lost it, But the biggest step I did...Which changed me.Which tell me actually what I want... However, still those memories are there for those I cry...I cry badly...If you want to know them ask my pillows...They know me well...Ask my lips touching that cigarette. Ask my heart, which beats for faster after seeing fail in the result card.

I just fed with the words of parents, friends, relatives and from this society. And then died.

After my death:

They all are thinking why I did this to me. However, they are not at all realizing that they all collectively involved killing me. When I'm in pain, no one is there for me. After my death, all cries that why you left me alone. However, when I'm alone no one is there. Before death, my soul is rest in Pisces and after death my soul rest in peace.

My soul wanted only one thing to say. Understand the people who want to be a torchbearer for their family, for new generation. They may not succeed immediately, but they will definitely. He or she may succeed at some point of time when he or she is alive. Don't kill your child at a cost of your prestige in the society by your words.

Ritobrata Das

Hello it's Ritobrata here doing mechanical engineering but following something important only to me.

Someone born with wings,
Someone develops them,
Someone learns to improvise,
Someone grows with time
but don't worry.
Time will come,
When you will rise.
Showing everyone your worth,
But never over shadow other with it.

Submission 2

It's sun job to shine,
It's wind job to blow.
But it's solely my job to think about you...!!!
But it's solely my job to think about you...!!!

Samriddhi Gupta

Hello everyone my name is Samriddhi Gupta and I am an avid reader. I am a 17-year-old with many dreams and one of them being publishing my own book someday. One of my many inspirations include Gina Lenetti - the human form of the 100 emoji. The works that I have submitted are truly written from my heart and I hope you have a fulfilling read.

Voices

 I can't find myself in this crowd
The voices in my head are too loud
My ego and jealousy always get the best of me
baby I don't know what these voices can be.
Everything has a reason
But honey my love for you is only a treason.
My heart sinks every time I think about you.
Knowing that the fantasy of you and I can never be true
There's no one to trust
All my hopes transform to dust,
All I feel now is hopelessness and despair.
Screaming on the top of my lungs and tearing my hair
I just asked you to be sincere,
but my doubts have now turned to fears.
The voices tell me to surrender and
never remember the people I loved the most
cause now they are All ghosts.
Was fitting in meant to be Everything,
I have lost the meaning of a human being,
the mind is like a moth drawn to a flame
Killing itself to win the name fame
and the cursed game.
Stop please, stop these.
Voices have put me in a trance.
I couldn't even recognize myself in the thousandth glance
My head controls my heart,
Tearing my body apart
Feeling so numb in the violent pain
Trapped in the burning chains.
Raging a cry of help and freedom
from this mind slaughter.
Was it a sin to love somebody's daughter?

To end this strife.
My voices are vice.
A farewell and a bow.
It all end NOW.

The divine

What do you see when you look up at the night sky?

I see you because you are not a creature of land you are the most magnificent work of the almighty that could have touched me with the gentlest hands. But as you go with the night, I'll always remember you in the deepest part of my soul.

She smelled of jasmine and clove and felt like a cool summer breeze. Nargis was the most enchanting and breathtaking goddess that ever-set foot on the face of earth. A mystic creature indeed,

I met Nargis when I was 16 the age where innocence ripens into maturity. She captured my eye at the first instance when I saw her at the louvre and out of all the art, I only could admire her. She was an architecture student and loved her work. We were soon acquainted and became fast friends she was all I could dream about. But there was one thing more terrifying than the nightmares that made her tremble at night and it was the fear falling in love. I did not crumble the sheets at night when she screamed helplessly but I was right there lying beside her to show her that I was there with her for every step, day and night to comfort her in my arms. Our home was not a beautiful Palace or an epitome of beauty but a simple white washed house along the streets of Paris. Her shadow gleamed by the light of the half-lit cigarette. A Ray of light creeped into our room every dawn to make us admire the sweet release of dusk. She never woke up with jolts but shivered and mumbled in her sleep". You listen to me not with your ears and for I do not speak with this mouth, but I ask you to hear me and view me from the deep depths of your despaired soul". She slowly broke into a stream of tears and as I pulled her closer to my heart as I could feel the thumping of her chest against mine, we both knew that at that moment we could not be more in love. I slowly whispered in her ear as she tucked her hair behind it the scent of cinnamon aroused my senses and the winter breeze blew her hair, I vowed to her that I would love and cherish her till the end of time.

A completely different and exciting journey was in front of us as we travelled to the most distant places on earth to feel the tranquility and calmness of the ocean while glancing at the ever-graceful moon. And on some days, we would ignite our wild spirits and jump from the highest peaks in Switzerland to dipping ourselves in the icy cold water of the dead sea. From surrendering ourselves to the craziest and most beautiful adventures we found ourselves. We had smelt the beautiful sunset of ibiza and heard the bazaars of Hyderabad and tasted the snowflakes as they trinkled down our faces. But all good times must end like this one too when we reached back to our paradise, we discovered several letters disclosing the death of Nargis's only father. She poured her eyes out at the end now she had no one left in this world whom she could blindly trust and fall back for the more difficult times that still haunted her. She didn't wake up that night to smoke her cigar or to stare at the endless ocean of possibilities but said " I don't want to wake up, If I do then this nightmare will never end and I might wake up in Baghdad or Syria". I could not do anything but patiently look at the dying autumn of October and the most mortal deity that lay close beside me.

Her breath was like a spree of 'itra' and her hair shined with the with the aesthetic golden-brown color of a surreal sunset. Her veins made me travel to the deepest parts of her soul. I had never felt such true bliss Nargis was and always will be the woman of my dreams and seeing her become into an even beautiful human being fulfilled the purpose of my life. She was in fact a true goddess in the form of an undeniably irresistible Arabic beauty.

WHY?

Why can't I breathe
when there's air all around?
Maybe my head just hit the hard ground.
Why can't I see when there's light everywhere?

Maybe because we are blind to see
the power of love and care Why does everything look real
when it's fake
Are we giving back how much we take?

Why can't we show love show compassion
When we have hearts made to feel
Is this the real deal?

Why can't we just pause and be thankful for this life Honey,
because we don't live, we just survive
Why does hatred have to end?

Can't our pride and ego bend
So, be grateful for the life you have been given
Because it's all about the small joys that are hidden.

Upen Reddy

Upender Reddy Kanukula, A banker by profession, is artistically inclined ever since his childhood. His works have been featured in Reflections W&R Mag, festivalforpoetry.com, handwritten.com and Lakdi-ka-pul-the poetry bridge, a collection of poems by poets of Twin City Poetry Club. He is heavily influenced by the creative works of & quot; David Ogilvy & quot, any time you feel blue, he will motivate you and lighten your spirits.

Bygones be bygones

Don't keep me away from poetry
but keep me away from people
Don't keep me away from the observations of my eye
but keep me away from the effects of those observations.

Don't keep away from absorbing others pain,
But keep me away from my unknown anger forever.
Don't keep away from me,
But keep away from my slight darker side

Tonight,
Emotions I can't hide I abide,
To the pain Slowly it subsides and divides.

Into pros and cons,
slowly the reader yawns,
saying "bygones be bygones".

Subhashini Natarajan

She is a half open window constantly trying bleed ink onto the blank pages of life.

The smashed window

Behind the smashed window,
Who is there looking at me struggle in life?
Besides the great light that is being reflected upon the
sky,
Why am I still seeing the broken pieces,
mirroring my shattered dreams?

Who is there painting my sky with invisible hands
letting me breathe in eternity?
Long beyond the clutching grasp of my hand,
Why is my quivering innermost thought slipping away?
Seeing the broken pieces of glass,
Bleeding my own rays.

Letting it shimmer in an array of constellations,
Entangled,Snarled, Entwined,
After denying myself for a long period,
Peeling off the mask,
I glow so brightly in the haunted chapel of my mind.
Breathing in my passion.

Sharayu Salunkhe

Hi, I am 23 years old, an avid reader and writing enthusiast. I am from Mumbai. And I love to write.

It was all a lie

You amble towards the door,
and hold the cold knob,
To open the door wide, and walk away,
Like forever from my life.

While I try to clasp,
That cold knob,
With my body quivering, and voice choking,
I resist you,
From biding goodbye, but you whisper,
"It was all a lie".

And make me shake,
From the alluring dreams,
Of togetherness I had espied,
So, I try to hold you,
In my embrace.

Maybe for the last time, but you deny,
And walk from the door,
While I stand and, watch you fade away,
from my teary eyes,
leaving back the echoes,
"It was all a lie".

Nostalgia and You

Half lost, half lonely
Eyes filled till the brim
Holding a glass of agony
I stare at the door
In front of me blankly
Without moving my eyes.
"How long has it been?"
I hear his mellifluous voice;
I have been craving
To get on since long....

I turn around to look at his face,
that alluring smile,
And his gleaming eyes....
Shifted the aura of my soul
and everything else around.
I give him a mystifying look.
"How long have you been looking at this door?"
He asks again.

I stutter a bit and mumble
"Since the day you left,
three years and fifty-six days to be precise."
Nostalgia hits me again
and I find myself drenched in tears.
He sits next to me,
Holds my face in his palms and whisper
"When do you plan to move on?"

I look in his eyes and mutter
"I have been relentlessly
Looking at this door to open
For days, weeks and months

This door opened quite a few times
And I have seen some blur faces Coming down.
But none of them was yours.

Now, I have made a pact with myself,
I will stay grounded,
Stare at this door,
until I see the face
Walking through the door Is yours again."

Pen, paper and you

"And do you write about all the guys you meet?" He asks me, lighting his cigarette. "Or just say, how many guys have you wrote about?" "Not many", I tell him. "I wrote about just one guy to be precise. Others, I was never able to carve into words and put on paper." "And what made you write about him?" He asks me again offering his cigarette. I hold the cig and take a deep puff that fills my lungs, I close my eyes and his images flicker in front of me. I sigh a bit and say, "Love and pain is what made me write about him".

He takes my palm in his and asks, "Will you ever write about me?"

I take a deep breath and begin, "The guy I wrote about, have been too handsome, who with his presence changed the complete aura around, making me feel loved for long moments I had spent with him, but the other moment he bequeathed perpetual pain. You are too handsome too, and I can carve you into words, words put into sentences that will describe how my heart skips a beat every time you look at me with those glinting eyes and how I steal glances when you take that smoke within you with those parted lips. You make me feel loved now. And all the guys whom I have loved, who made me feel loved and who have seen my scars have left me, and now that you have seen them as well someday or the other, you will leave me too, drowning me again in the ocean of relentless pain? And certainly, I will write about you, your charm, your love and pain, from the day you abandoned my heart."

Neha Mandal

Neha Mandal lives in a small city of Jorhat situated in Assam. She is of seventeen years who is passionate about writing as she believes that she has a god gifted power of framing her emotions into poetries. She is a student of Humanities studying in 12th standard in Assam Rifles public school of Jorhat zilla. She's a stage performer, an open mic speaker and even a singer too. Her aim is to explore herself at a great extent and enjoy her entire life with different experiments with herself because she doesn't only want to earn money.

Ak khoobsurat si Nari

Pata nai ye kesi khubsurti he
Ha ! Pata nahi ye kesi khobsurti he unki ,
Jo sabko khubsurat banati he ,
Abang badsurti ko bhi khubsurti me badalneka
upay rakhti he .
Esi shakti he unke pass jo sabko ,
Jiban ki sacchai sikhlati he .
Bo datti jaroor mujhe ,
Mere har ek galat kadam pe . (2)
Taki me chal saku hamesha
Sacchai ki rah pe .
Bo haat na chorti mera kabhi ,
Khari reheti mere sath ;
Mere haar ek kathinaiyon me.
Larna toh sikhaya he unhone mujhe
Aur jeetne ko banadi meri majboori ,
Taki zindagi me kabhi mushkil
Naho mujhe mere akelepan me .
Bo koi bari hasti toh nahi ,
Balki hamari hi tarah
Ek sadharan si he Nari
Lekin asadharan karname
Karti nazar ati he –
Bo he mere 'Dil' ke bohot kareeb ,
Jo mere Dil ko sun samajh leti he ;
Mere kuch na kehene par bhi .
Bo pyaar karti mujhse bohot
Aur pyaar karna bhi sikhlati he .
Bo he 'Bhagban' saman
Aur ek sheetal hriday bhari Nari .
Bo he thori alag iss bheed se,

Aur thori Nirali mere hisabse ,
Kyunki bo aur koi nahi
Maa he meri .

LOVING EACH OTHER

One who makes me smile,
With whom I would walk a mile.
His eyes have a unique spark,
which is up to the mark.
He is very cute and simple,
with a face that has a dimple.
In my sadness,
He reminds me of happiness.
Seeing him in pain,
Is worse than a sprain.
Small things give him pleasure and joy,
this makes me over joy.
He is so close,
That I chose not to be disclose.

Srashti Srivastava.

This is Srashti Srivastava. I am a student of MBA. My journey of writing started when I was in class seventh, and the reason behind me being able to write from beginning itself is my father - Late Mr. Sharda Prasad Srivastava

आज मैं अपनी कलम से कुछ लिखना चाहती हूँ,

देश के प्रति अपने भावो को, कलम की सहायता से व्यक्त करना
चाहती हूँ,

बढ़ती हुई महंगाई, रोज़ - रोज़ की आतंकवादी लड़ाई,

देश के बच्चों का डूबता भविष्य और ना जाने कितने ही हैं जिसे
अपने देश मे बढ़ने पर विराम लगाना चाहती हूँ ।

अपने देश की व्यंगात्मक स्थिति को सिरे से मिटाना चाहती हूँ ।

देश की प्रतिकूल व्यवस्थाओं को, नेताओं के बेढंगे व्यवहार को
अनुकूल बनाना चाहती हूँ,

पिछड़े हुए लोगों की पिछड़ी हुई सोच को, आज की सोच से
मुखातिब कराना चाहती हूँ,

रूठी हुई सोने की चिड़िया के रुख को वापिस घुमाना चाहती हूँ ।

अपने देश की बिगड़ी हुई सीरत को फिर से बदलना चाहती हूँ ।

Aarti Shahdadpuri

Aarti Shahdadpuri is just a beginner to the "World of Writers." She is Currently in third year of financial markets, degree college. Her spirit is wild and free. She is cheerful with bright and hopeful eyes. At last she is splendid cornucopia of love and Emotions. Instagram -letthewords_speak, sweek application -aarti_shahdadpuri

Her Id- https://www.facebook.com/aarti.shahdadpuri}

The guardian angel

24 December 2018,

Like every beautiful morning, I was glancing out the window and cherishing the peaceful breeze. It was winter. The foggy mornings were soothing the hearts of everyone. Everything was covered by the white blanket of the snow. Children were playing with the snow balls, throwing it at each other. I miss those days where I use to go with my Granno (grandfather) and do a lot of fun too.

On my left side of the window, I saw some people were roaming by holding the Cello, Violin in hands and playing the Accordion along. I was wondering what they were celebrating unless I heard the song "Carol of bells" being played somewhere nearby. Guess that suggested 'The Christmas'. They halted at my door step and asked for some contribution for celebration of Christmas night grand. I was super excited to be the part of it. I rushed for the main door to greet them until mom came back with some donation. "How wonderful it feels to celebrate such days!" I said to mom. Seeing me so joyful, mom said "Yes darling, do you remember last year when you wrote a wish to Santa? I replied, "Oh Yes! Mom, I completely forgot that. I will do the same this year as well, I will catch you later. I need to make a long wish list for the Santa."

I went to my room and took out my glitter pens and a plain paper to write all that my heart wishes.
After thinking all my favorite stuff that proved unnecessary. I came to a conclusion that these are   not the right things to be asked from Santa Claus. But then, looking beyond the silly things I wish at every Christmas.vThere was one person whom I miss the most

but never show and whom I loved more than anybody but never uttered a single word. Who made me what I am today? To the one who has taught me the meaning of unconditional love. The only one who kept me safe by showing me the betrayal of the outside world.

My granno (grandfather).

I decided to write a letter to him because he was my only Santa until last Christmas.

"Dear Granno,

Life has left a vacuum without you which has always made me felt at unease. All these days without you seem less complete.
I miss you the most, you always felt like roof of the home and the roots of plants. You have always been the saviour.
I still remember the childhood days; I have lived with you. Whenever I got my results, I came rushing to you with all the smiles and giving you a bear hug. I used to happily ask for my rewards. I held your hand and walked the dark streets of life which had always made me stronger and bolder. From learning to cook for you to bringing food for you at uninvited hospitals; life taught me different meanings. Whenever I get any compliments regarding the personality I carry or the person I have become: my heart feels- they all compliment you. Cause I am less of me and more of you. I relate myself deeply to you.
You have been the person who has read my eyes, understood my hidden tears and of course the gulped words. In your existence I was a free bird reaching heights in the sky, but without you I have been the bird who doesn't wish to fly anymore? I wonder why lord parted us away. Belonging from same path, God diversified our

roadways. I feel alone in this wicked world. The walls of our home never let me feel your absence.
From telling you about the day I spent, to wishing I could tell you how the whole year went.

The old melodies, we use to sing along are now in my heart. And I sing them like old days hoping to hear your singing voice, next to mine. Though I know it's never going to happen again. I sing them to cherish your presence in your undeniable absence. Today when I stand with a mic in my hand to perform a piece, all that I do is tell the universe about you. I wish you could witness it too. Being your little girl to growing up so fast. Treasuring my art and encouraging me to keep going. My heart craves for your existence. My words want your ears to listen. My unsecured world wishes to live in the safe guard completed by you. I want to tell you how much my heart holds love for you. From the day you took my care, to the days I took care of you, we lived all the phases of life together. When I tell people that I wish to have a converse again with you, they label me insane and tell me it is impossible. I wish to show them that how I still have you. I can talk to you in the dreams I envision. In the decisions I make, which are taught by you. Though it's the fact that you are not around, But deep down my heart knows you never really left me. I have you now, I will have you forever.
You are being missed my beloved Granno.

I ended the letter and kept it inside my favorite red sock, keeping it beneath his photo frame. I went to the church where the Christmas celebrations were going, everyone was so happily dancing and enjoying the night. And I was happy in a hope that the letter would reach to my Great Old man."

Dev Jhawar

A happy go lucky guy.

Casual writer. Aspirant of Hotel Management.

Food and cricket are love while sleep and sarcasm are bae.

इरादों में अभी भी क्यों इतनी जान बाकी है,
तेरे किए वादों का इम्तिहान भी बाकी है,
अधूरी क्यों रह गई तुम्हारी यह बेरुखी,
अभी दिल के हर तुकड़े में तुम्हारा नाम भी बाकी है।

Sneha Tiwari

A doctor by profession and a literary blogger by passion. With her proses and poetry, she touches the tides, high or low: of the society and nature around. To her, writing is to explore the inner consciousness. She strikes the keys of the souls of the readers with her simple, yet captivating and relative commentary. She has been previously published in the "Lakdi Ka Pul-II" Dive into her works on: www.drsnehatiwari155.wordpress.com

कैसे मानूं ये जुदाई तेरी मेरी/ how to believe कैसे मान लूं दिल तुम्हारा कभी धड़का न होगा , कैसे मान लूं , यादें तड़पाती न होंगी कभी तुम्हें । कैसे मान लूं जो हाल है मेरा यहाँ , वो हाल नहीं है तेरा वहाँ । कैसे मान लूं , पल जो जीये मैंने , संग मेरे वो जीये न होंगे तुमने , कैसे मान लूं जो ये रूठा है तू, अलविदा बोल चला है तू, निकला है दिल से ही तेरे । कैसे मान लूं तू वो नहीं अब , जिस से मिली थी मैं कभी, कैसे मान लूं खुश है तू बिछड़ के मुझसे वहाँ , जब खुश नहीं मैं बिछड़ के तुझ से यहाँ ।

English translation:

How to believe

How to believe your heart never miss it's beat like mine did, how to believe you don't get affected by memories like I do. How to believe you are not at same place, where I am. How to believe the moments I live, never existed for u. How to believe your bye forever, came from your heart only, how to believe you are not the one I met before. How to believe you are happy there, when I am not happy here.
P.S.- In context of a pain to be left alone all of sudden.

The Mirror

I saw you flourishing your beauty in front of me,
Combing your hair beautifully,
smiling with confidence, loving yourself.
I remember the spark in your eye,
you grooming yourself to your best,
Dancing on music of surroundings,
Oh My God! you were so beautiful.

But this was never for me,

your beauty, your smile, your aliveness.

This was for someone else who brought love in your life,

but I love you too, and will always till my last breath,

For I am because of you.
But it has been days, you don't come near to me now.
I had not seen your smile, spark in your eyes, any aliveness
near.
I see you from a distance now, lying there, lost in
thoughts,
Tears rolling down your cheeks, seems you stopped living
now. Why?
Does someone else always needed to make you feel
loved?
Can't you do that to you,
can't you live and relish what you have on your own,
can't you dance alone in your solitude,
can't you sing along with birds out there?
I always see you; I am always there with you,
Even in your lonesome,
I make you look the real beauty lying within you,

I always admire it and will love to admire it more with you.
The Mirror miss you badly, please come back.

Manali Debroy

Manali, is an ambitious person who is an MBA by education and a banker by profession but a writer at heart. She has been a writer since her six-year-old self-started writing letters to her grandfather which just made her fall in love with words and their power of communicating. She has published her first book, 'Twist and turns of life' - a poetry collection which is available in Amazon. She writes about multiple themes and topics but mostly driven by realistic fiction and motivational thoughts.

Just Another day (prose)

The window swings by the rustling wind;
the door mat gets drenched by the crazy downpour;
the dog keeps barking in the same direction,
At something or someone who knows!

The beggar sits beneath that lam post every day,
but never asks for money, who knows why!
I see people rushing past each other;
more like bees, than humans,
and I walk down the street thinking,
It's just another day!

The woman in the corner shop only seems to care about
waving away the flies,
I wonder if that's her job or her way to pass time.
The baby next door is always happy and dancing around in
their garden,
I wonder if all the babies are the same or is this one the
happiest.
The couple across the street kisses each other every
morning before she goes to work,
and at midday I see them kissing again
but her resemblance is not the same,
I wonder if the wife comes again in the guise of another
woman!
Crossing the home decor shop,
I stand and look for me in their large mirror displayed
outside,
I see a faint me and then I close my eyes
And in my mind, I think again,
It's just another day!

A paper boat (short story)

Someone once told me that 'Life is like a paper boat. It sails per the waves or submerges to high tides.' What an analogy - comparing a human life with a paper, or is it with the boat? I sat all through the day trying to write this article on 'The human life - a paper boat'. But I couldn't fit my thoughts to compare a human with a paper boat. Even a boat is sailed through the storm and against the currents by a human, then why it submerges to high tides? Isn't a human capable of breaking all the impossibilities and carving out new possibilities? But then I also remember how vulnerable our race is to simple things in life like emotions. Like a sudden door slam when that someone walks out leaving us fragile to the core. Like the sudden death of that someone creates a void in our life leaving us trembling of the loneliness. That makes me think how such strong and the best creation of god, created for inventions and new creativity is so fragile that breaks down under the heaviness of emotions which is palpable to the mind and soul. And then I thought to pen down 'The human life - a paper boat', because it's not the impossibilities that we can't defy but it's the tensions between the heart and the soul we succumb to. After all the high tides in life only come when we are emotionally the weakest.

Naman Srivastava

I am a class 12th student who wants to become an engineer and a writer too.

Tensed, frightened and crying,
How we enter the home name 'hostel'. Everyone is just a stranger.
Journey begins within those four walls, what we do is just cry and cry.
The silence reminds us of our family.
Today also, mom called and asked about food, but today she is unaware Whether I ate or not?
Everyone asked whether I was fine?
But only I know what actually I was going through.
Strangers became friends, Migrants became local,
Sadness turned into happiness,
Suddenly environment changed. Crying face turned into a smiling one.
Silent hostel turned into a happy home. Now all became brothers.
Different caste, different religion, all became one.
Now we became family.
Shouting, hooting and celebrations all started in that happy home. Time passed and we started creating memories,
Some of them were freeze in camera too.
Time came when family was about to break,
Everyone was sad remembering those moments spent together. This was something more than a heartbreak.
We entered and left hostel with a crying face.
And now again the whole world seems to be a stranger again.

Himanshi Tanwar

Himanshi is the daughter of Mr. Tejpal Singh and Mrs. Babita. I am from Palwal, Haryana. Right now, I am pursuing B. Com Hons. I keep positive attitude towards my life. I love every work that I do. I have interest in reading novels, which inspires me a lot and touches my soul. I really want to become a Novelist one day. I want to touch the sky but at the same time.

Let today be the day,
I live for everyone!
Let today be the day,
I dream for ourselves!
Let today be the day,
I made a forever promise to you!
Let today be the day,
I talk to my soul!

Let today be the day,
I listen to my heart!
Let today be the day,
We create a perfect picture!
Let today be the day,
I hope for a better tomorrow!

Let today be the day,
I pray for you!
Let today be the day,
You feel blessed to have me in your life!!!

Nimmi, born in God's own country is a Blogger and a HR by profession. She is passionate about nature, painting and music. A Writer by Day and a Reader by night. She has written over 150 poems on feelings and emotions and has been an active participant in word press writing challenges since last three years. In her free time, she likes being with her family and enjoying every moment of life as it comes. You can follow her at feelingsoulmates.wordpress.com

I'm captive in a golden cage,
Beautiful things filling my life's page,
But a cage is still a cage.
Where I'm struggling at this stage,
Finding the ways to fly, Again, in that lovely blue sky,
Birds are in a cage, never sings, but in reality, they cry,
Some way or another,
We are all living in a cage, Our own golden cage.
Some got tired and compromised, some are still trying to
get recognized,
We have to hold on to our dreams,
Cause, if dreams die
We will never come out and fly.
Freedom is an everlasting hope,
So, try and cope,
Break out this locked up door,
Come out and roar.

Harish Labana says

Writing is my passion, and I'm student of B.Sc. Computer Science, From Udaipur Rajasthan, and am 18 years old,

"My favorite Line -- Never trust your fears, they don't know your strength".

Whenever I see you,
There is always a hope of "My Life",
With your Smile and Laugh,
My face always shines with, A naughty smile,
Because, My life is dependent on "Your Smile".

My World starts from You,
And Ends at you.
This time I'm serious,
I am serious about you.
I swear, okay, look,
In my eyes and see,
If you think that I am lying,
You can go,
Love my choice and Kills by Profession.

Khushi Bano Nadri

Hi! I am Khushi Bano Nadri and I am a Science student from Seth Anandram Jaipauria School, Kanpur. Writing poems, lyrics and short stories is my passion.

Gratitude to Maa

When there's nobody there,
I see you standing by my side,
At times to me the world seems murky
but you bring a gleam of hope,
when people don't believe in my abilities,
You are the one who gets back my confidence,
While the world is too busy,
pointing out my flaws,
you are the one to show the path of perfection,
it's you maa who understands me the most,
It's you maa who loves me the most,
Nothing can service what all you have done for me
'Maa'.

"Materiality of the world "

When you look up in the sky,
Aren't you lost in the fantasy world?
The stars twinkle and the moon shines,
looking at them, don't you feel light?
All joy fades
under the superficial glory of materialistic world.
We are lost in the dull, lead like world.
And the twinkling stars and shinning moon does not
seem gold.

"Urgent need for a tranquil world "

Why can't I live in a tranquil world?
People running behind the fake glory of avaricious world,
People boasting about the things they possess.
Why can't life be easy and simple?
Why can't I live in a tranquil world?
People having either superiority or inferiority complex,
mocking each other.
Why can't people mind their own business?
Why people draw lines
when it comes to serve the ones in need?
Are they blind to the gesture of kindness?
Why can't I live in a tranquil world?

There is no answer to my question because there is a fear in people to accept that there's somebody above writing their mistakes.

Anjali Chandak

Student. Aspiring Writer. This is my first writeup.

I have a story,
A story to influence everyone here.
A story to inspire people to claim attraction as love.
A story of me, a story with him.
Here,
The new year's beginning, bought a change in my life.
A change I never thought would take place.
A change that gifted me him.
A change that made me fall again,
A change that rebuilt my trust over love.
A love of voice, a love of waiting.
A love that I admired. A love that I love.
We've been together for something good,
For something which every young mind awaits.
We've been together for the destiny wants us to be,
Unknowingly we met, for a reason.
We've been together for the love that still remains
incomplete,
For we're the players in this world.
For we're the players confusing the god of love.
For the Cupid wanted to be.
We've been together,
For the conflicting thoughts.
We've together because everything in this world seems
different when it's with you.
Then why not stay together forever?

Akshita Agarwal

I am a 23-year-old young girl who is passionate about writing. I write with pseudo name Womika Goyal when I write stories, snippets, musings etc. in English. I am also a poet with pseudo name 'Jheel'. Besides I am an entrepreneur and a teacher. I am also powering my masters in commerce. Belonging to a business class family I have always been passionate about business. My father, Mr. Dinesh Agarwal, a business man, is my inspiration. My mother, Mrs. Krishna Agarwal, a home maker, deserves all the credit for my writing skills. One can wish me on 21/06/96.

3 Years in 3 Days

It was the Christmas cum reunion party; a total of 3-day event. School grounds were supposed to be the venue but being located in a small town, our premises lacked facilities and so the venue was changed. I was too excited about the event as the invitation mentioned "with spouse" and also it had been 15 years we were matriculated.

Being the last one probably to reach the venue I could see almost 148 heads laughing and talking. Amit and I had added to it – 150. I could see engineers, doctors, MBAs, officers and may more all be standing under one roof. Some of us were parents including me. Everything seemed so different. The only person whom I was in constant contact was Mann.

The event that evening was a test. The event management team had set up the almost exact replica of our school exam hall. The question sheet had 75 questions – one question related to one student from our school days. Now I know why we were asked to submit a set of 10 questions related to us from our school days along with the confirmation form.

I glanced around the hall immediately after I was done just to find the seat. Number 73, the number which I had skipped purposefully I the answer sheet was vacant. None of us had left the hall. While we wrote this test, our spouses were enjoying 'Tambola' and tea. That night we had our dinner round the bonfire and went to sleep as most of us were tired with the journey.

Next morning, the scene of the school canteen was set for the breakfast and so was the menu. 'Tell a tale' was on and everyone was laughing, talking about the past. I was happy to see Amit get along
well with my batch mates. 'Tug of war', 'Antakshari',

'Dumsheras', musical chair were the events of the day. We relived our school days in 'tic-tac-toe' and 'dot to dot' line games.

Finally, it was Christmas. Amit had left for breakfast along with my friends and I walked alone to the hall only to see 'him' in the crowd. I stared at him, standing in his olive-green shirt and black denims with a black coat—dressed formally like I had always wanted him to. My gaze was disturbed by Amar as he offered me breakfast from his plate and informed me that the skit on Jesus' birth was about to begin in about 15 minutes and that I should hurry. After the skit and Santa's dance, we had lunch and returned to our rooms to get ready for the evening. Throughout the events I could not resist my eyes from staring at him but we did not speak even a single word to each other. As per the invite, females were dressed in red and male were in black for the evening. I had worn the fish tail scarlet gown like he had wished to see me. In the evening, the test results of the first day test were announced. The event manager announced paper dance, balloon dance and other games for the couple. After these, he made an announcement which flushed my cheeks red and filled the hall with hooting. My husband had wished to see me dance with the boys who once had crush on me and was supported by all the wives (batch mates' wives). After many comments and cheers, finally Amar, Abhishek and Vineet stepped forward. We had a gala time while we were dancing. Everyone but Waman stepped forward to dance with me who was finally pushed forward by Amit. The evening passed. The three days were over. We left with hampers as token of reunion.

I could see him standing there alone among the crowd. By the time lunch was over Waman and I had not spoken a word but exchanged glances. Soon I received a letter that made those 3 years flash back in my brain. The letter read:

"Dear Nirja (Niru),

I was glad to see you and was happy to know that you are a mother now. Don't worry, I am a businessman but sorry I could not be what you wished me to be. My fashion is your gift and I shall never discard it. Seeing me single everyone has been consoling me that every love story does not have a happy ending but I know that mine has been a happy one. You are happy with Amit and I am happy for you; that makes us both happy making it a happy ending. I don't blame you for these years and want you to stop blaming yourself for whatever had happened 8 years ago. Amit is the best man for you.

Yours,

Waman"

My concentration was broken with the sound of the cough. I looked around to see my mailman, my husband standing there. I hugged him tight in agreement with the last line of the letter. Amit never read that letter but gifted me the three years in his wish to see me dance with my lovers and I know by this gesture of his how much he loves and trusts me.

High Profile

It was grey. The clouds roared while she was dancing her happy dance on the result day. She was a graduate now. "The girl was hit with the car. The driver ran away leaving the victim to die in the pool of blood.... The sources report a missing gold ring which according to victim's family was worn by the victim on her left hand. The investigation of the case is pacing fast." The thunder struck her when she was introduced to Kunal, immediately after she had stepped in with the results. Kunal was the chosen prospective groom for her by her brother. She was asked to get ready as fast as possible as all the preparations for the ring ceremony had been made and she was the only one being waited for. "The hit and run case are again on the talks. The culprit has been arrested on Thursday. Sources informed that according to the statement of the accused, the victim Neerja Singh aged 21 jumped in front of his car...." The bright yellow saree contradicted the sky. Like a doll, she was decorated and made to sit next to Kunal. 'Doll's marriage' was the game being played with the slightest difference of the doll being alive in this case. The rings were exchanged and the commencement of the ceremony marked the winding up of her dreams. Kunal had promised her that he made sure that she completed her studies even after marriage.

"After the guilt's arrest the police were about to wrap up the investigation of Neerja Singh hit and run case. But her family is not letting the case to be closed. They want the police to investigate further and recover the lost gold ring. They have even filed a suit against the Doctors and the hospital with the charges of theft...."

She spent hours talking to Kunal over phone. The post engagement period - she had known Kunal 'enough' to write an essay of 200 words on him. In this post engagement phase, she had learnt to cook all his favorite dishes and other household chores which she was not required to be good at as she would have servants to do them. A rich husband who even cared for her studies and career, pampered her with gifts and is understanding- what else does a woman need? "Mr. Kunal Singh, the chairman of Singh Group of Industries has been arrested. Sources say he is now among the prime suspects in the hit and run case of Neerja Singh...."

It had been three months after her marriage. Even today the sky is grey. The color of her saree again contradicted the sky that day. Limping in pain she came out of the kitchen with a tray and a smile on her face. Purple ornamented her that day. "The high-profile case of Neerja Singh is finally closed. The High Court verdicts Mr. Kunal Singh guilty of domestic violence and tempering with the proofs. The license of the Doctors involved with Mr.Singh has also been cancelled. The case was solved by the statement given by Mahesh, the ward boy..."

Today finally Niru had restored enough courage to take the decision of fleeing away. She had a new life growing inside her whom she wanted to give birth. She had decided she won't let her husband kill the baby girl inside her womb. Hurrying down the street in the darkness of night drenched in rain, she limped in pain to save herself. She had left the gold ring on the dressing table; the ring that held her like a chain. Luckily for Kunal, the baby girl died even before being born to earth. Purple still adorned her body. The driver was behind the bars for not helping Neerja and was also accused of killing one life but nature knew that actually it was two.

(Editor)

Mahak Sharma

Mahak Sharma is a graduate from Delhi university. She is currently pursuing her masters in English literature. Writing provides her with the liberty of imagination. She sincerely thanks her parents for the constant support and says that "Next to God, thy parents." (William Penn). She mentions that,' Writing to me is a part of what doesn't always exist but sometimes I can make it real. It detoxifies the mind of the raw strings of wounds and relieves the soul.'

Preferences

It sounds ridiculous but only I feel productive
when I'm doing nothing. Sitting back, just relaxing.
Popping blue beans, burning bowls of green.
And just thinking.
Daydreaming about how things could have been.
How things could still be,
But how things will probably be,
Just close your eyes and let music be your guide.
Entire lives constructed and played out in grand fashion.
A world so detailed
I would rather get lost,
And never come back to this travesty of a society,
so raw and primal.
so human.
My world is so beautiful and yet so depressing
because it's what ours could be,
but never will become.
Anything to distract me from this.
The twenty-one-year-old burnout
grinding through life because there aren't many options left.
So where will I be in 5 years?

Vedika beriwal

Vedika Beriwal, an 18-year-old Commerce Student from Dibrugarh -Assam- India. Currently studying at VKV Dibrugarh, an ex-student of Shree Agrasen Academy. Knitting words and expressing what I think through writing gives me immense pleasure. I don't write everyday neither I detach myself completely from writing. I keep my work simple and easy to catch.

A piece of my heart ~ Childhood

When I turn back,
I see the secret cards stored in the wooden box.
Fights for the only blue crayon among the lot.
The orange colored candies were able to bring smile on our
chubby faces.
We smiled confidently even with braces.
The pink blush on the cheeks were not fake.

We never hesitate to eat the whole one-pound cake.
Needs were fulfilled and wants were meaningless.
Clothes were hands stitched and hair a mess.
Enacting Mom gave me immense pleasure.
Love was pure and toys were the only treasure.
The secrets were unrevealed
and tears were never the end.
Then was the time of real magic,
Why can't the child inside us live forever and break the
trend!

Manshi Toshniwal
A 17-year-old, commerce student from Dibrugarh,
Assam. Daughter of Mahavir Toshniwal and Sarika
Toshniwal.
Currently studying in Salt Academy, an ex student of
Little Flower School.
Writing makes me and my soul happy!

That is the thing about me, I don't give up on people I love, easily and that is why I don't give up on you. It is really hard. But no matter how hard the situation becomes; my heart just doesn't want to let yours go. It is not easy to find a human like you. Your soul is purely dipped in honey as though it provides shelter for my venom. You make me happy without even trying to do so. You support me and motivate me. You're always there to catch me whenever I fall and when I hold your hands, literally everything in the world stops and I feel protected. You're my home. So, when you leave, trust me it is not going to be easy for me to forget you. Life is already hard and it is going to be hardest without you because I'm addicted to you and I forget that too much of an addiction isn't good. Without you, I'll be nothing. With you in everything. Now that you know that I don't give up, just know that when I do, trust me, you've lost everything.

MY PRIDE

My pride is my soul,
My soul is immortal,
Break this body,
I'll not ask for mercy.
Make me cry?
I would rather die.
Nothing is worth begging for, nothing;
Not money, not fame, not hunger,
not love, not life, nothing;

For my pride is there to guide me, to remind me;
There is no one greater in this world, than me;
No one will get the better of me,
Not while my pride holds me,
For am I not unlike God,
Made in his own image.

Anisha Chakraborty from Jorhat, Assam says I am 16 years old. I am a student of Science stream but also a poetry lover! Who says a Science student cannot love literature or poetries! Poetry is my loved side. My father always says that we should never leave our passion so here I am with my poem. Trying do my studies and poetries by giving equal time to both of them!

एक शाम जब मशगूल थी,
शाज़ा के एक किनारे पे।
देख रही थी, फूलों की खिलखिलाहट को।
सुन रही थी, भवरों की गुनगुनाहट को।
महसूस कर रही थी,
अपनी जादुई समा को।
वह वादिया कुछ बता रही थी,
वह दरख़्त कुछ कह रहा था।
सूर्य उनपे गोर फार्म रहा था,
प्रकाश उनको दे रहा था।
मैंने सूर्य को देखने की कोशिश की,
पर देख न सकी।
कई बार कोशिश की और मायूस हो गई।
फिर मुझे आगाह हुआ कि,
सूर्य को देखते नहीं हैं, महसूस करते हैं!
ज़िंदगी के कुछ पल भी,
सूर्य की भाती होती हैं।
जिन्हें देखा नहीं जाता, जिया जाता हैं!

Sauhard Pandey

Sauhard Pandey an ardent fan of Mahendra Singh Dhoni! Wishes to become inspiring and great like his idol Mahi.

Ms. Dhoni the living legend

I don't know if this ever reaches you but half of my childhood has passed watching you make some maverick decisions that have paid off exceptionally well in the team's favour. No one has graced that space behind the stumps as much as you have.

It's been almost a decade since you first filled in the leader's shoes and began with a fairytale WT20 win.

There has been no stopping you. Those decisions of trusting Joginder Sharma in both semifinals as well as the finals showed us your courage and fearlessness as a captain.

In a nation where star cricketers are treated like Gods, you had the courage to take a bold decision by dropping stalwarts from the side who had been below par on the field.

In the field, you've rarely allowed emotions to get the better of you. In the most pressure situations, you've managed to keep your calm which has helped India pull off some splendid victories out of nowhere.

A great example of this can be the World Cup

finals. In spite of being out of form, you were brave enough to promote yourself above the man in form, in a match that the nation had waited for 28 long years. Knowing the consequences if the move might have backfired, you displayed a grit of fearlessness which a few might have dared to exhibit.

You've never shied away from taking unprecedented decisions.

Being selfless leads to extraordinary things. You've always put team's interest ahead of anything else. For years, you've donned the finishing role and promoted young talent up the batting order.

Anyways, Dear MSD,

It has been 14 years since you started playing cricket and in these 14 years you have come a long way. From being a flamboyant batsman, you are now the best FINISHER the cricketing world has ever seen. MAHENDRA SINGH DHONI is indeed a big name. Out of these 14 years I have been privileged to be a fan of yours for the last 13 years and let me tell you one thing in these 13 years you have given me countless to be proud of you. Yes, you may not be the same old M S

DHONI but your name is just enough to make bowlers shiver. From getting out on the first ball in your debut match to scoring 10,000+ ODI runs, you're now a living legend. You've made people change their phrases from "Sachin out hogaya hai abh TV bandh kardo" TO "Dhoni hai abhi bhi match khatam nahi hua hai" in these fourteen years.

You're the one to make India reach to such heights in cricket that we Indians could never even have dreamt of earlier. Each and every Indian is proud of you. You've shown the world that you can achieve your dreams no matter from which walk of life you're in.

Manasvi Parmar
16 years old from Kanpur. Writing has become a part of me, I can sometimes stop writing for a long time but I can never detach it from myself.
I believe, if the words used are correct and the feelings are real then the write-up will automatically find its audience.
Thanking Vedansh for always being there to help me regain my self- confidence.

Seems like she is full of joy

You saw her today in the garden,
plucking colorful flowers.
all she was doing was trying to collect those colors
back in her life.
oh, was she wearing a warm smile
when you passed by her at school.
She was hiding the pain that is breaking her deep
inside.
yes, she was reading a book about happiness in the
library yesterday.
she was learning how to be happy again.
was she writing something
while sitting on the last bench in the chemistry class?
hiding it from her friends?
what if I tell you that it wasn't a love letter for her crush
but a suicide note?
she smokes a lot these days, yes.
no, she isn't getting spoiled up; she is trying to die.
is she asking you to hang out with her someday?
truth is, she is trying to open up again.
and if I tell you that she is full of joy, I bet you'll believe
it.

Rashmithakapuganti is 23 years old, a girl from vizianagaram. She is an Interior Designer. She wrote motivational blogs; she was a bookaholic. Her dream is to inspire all people who have negative mindset& to throw out their negative thoughts and motivate them to achieve grand success in life.

A little girl's tale

Mom where are my paint brushes. Have you seen anywhere?
(Mom became like Google in the house for all misplace things)
Search in your shelf Swecha!
No mom it's not visible for me.
(Dad voice raised Hyndhavi, I am in an important call, please talk slowly)
 Mom I got my Camlin paint brushes Swecha raised her voice!
Swecha holds the brushes and feeling the smooth hair of brushes on her finger, just like a mom seeing his just born baby. Few years ago, I hold a pencil to write quotes but my mind diverted to an artist's way. I hold pencil & eraser to draw my feelings to paste on the book. Drawn so many and won so many prizes. My Mom & Dad supported a lot for me. I went to the National level for Painting competitions won medals.
My dream came true at the age of 12 years. I met so many famous artists. When I completed my 10th class dad said, my aim is to see u as Doctor, and serve the people. Daddy I want to become an Artist. I want to fulfil my dreams. I want to make my own way daddy. I don't want to be in this professional world. No... Swecha you have to leave these all artist skills. You should not hold brushes, paints, etc.... you have to do Doctor. "Don't design your life on paper, Design your life in patient's heart." What the sense made you to become an artist Swetha?
Dad! I can't hold the surgical scissors without heart. I will hold the paint brushes with heart. No, u have to listen to my words that're it no more arguments on this topic. Swecha went to her room. She saw her face in the mirror

and started to dislike herself. Why these parents won't agree with my life aim? Mom hugged her. Sweet heart don't cry. Situations will go on well don't cry.

Next-day morning Dad brought an application from college. Swecha, Come and fill this application! She took pen and removed the cap. Her tears turned into ink in the pen. Her words looked like blood marks. She filled the application and gave to her father. After one week, your college will be started, get ready, ok daddy, Because of you, I will go.

After one week, she joined in the college. One-day day mam gave records for drawing she completed all diagrams within a day where as her classmates can't even draw a single line. She used to help her friends in records. In her college, she got appreciations by seeing her work. She passed out her 12th with 98% and became state topper. After her 12th, She became busy in MBBS. She used to be happy outside but not inside.

One day her friend Rahul invited to his birthday party. All her friends planned to go. She wore Red frock smooth cloth, which feels smooth, kept cute feather earrings with silver plated, wore point heels with heavy white beads, by leaving hair loose she looks like angel. Her hair smells sweet more than her perfume She sat one side, and drawing doodles in the phone.

Her friend Rahul observed her and asked what are you doing here? No just like that replied Swecha. No, I'm observing you from first day why you are feeling lonely in your heart? She can't express her feelings directly to him. But she shared everything happened in her life with him. He felt depressed. They used to talk every day. Their friends took them as inspiration in their friendship. They both became best friends where someone can't come and fill their gap between them.

One-day, Rahul thought to give an unforgettable memory

throughout of life. Rahul called Swecha. Phone is ringing she attended the call. Swecha can we meet in beach at 4pm? Yeah... sure, I will be there at 4 pm. Her mind was running with a lot of thoughts why he is going to meet me? He wants to share any important matter with me? Time is 3 pm I have to get ready. She wore a white top with lace work and Jean's pant. with long earrings coated with pearls. She is very eager to meet him. She booked a cab and went to the beach.

Rahul, where are you? Swecha I will instruct you the way, please follow my instructions carefully. Ok I will follow. Come straight Take 1st left turn I will be there. After 10minutes, she rang to Rahul. I am here. Where are you? Rahul came and took him to one Hall where all people in the crowd.

She was surprised that she was in Painting competition. Swecha comes on to the Dias. A warm call from dignitaries on Dias. She stepped to the place where all dignitaries are there. Swecha is a wonderful artist, she has drawn a family love towards child she selected to Guinee's world Record & won first prize in State level. You are selected for the World Chersa Painting competition going to be held in London. She has no words for her grand success. Her family became proud of her. Her happiness endless.

End of the day, she called to Rahul. Really thank you so much for giving me a wonderful surprise. I was limitless in happiness. Rahul replied to You should say thanks to your dad. He called me 6months back and shared his love towards you. He searched all of your paintings your room and searched for best painting, and he contacted to all committee people presented today and arranged in exhibition.

I asked uncle why you're made her depressed in the age of 15yrs now why you are doing all these things? Rahul she is the best daughter. She left her passion because of my aim to become doctor. She sacrificed her interest towards art. This was the best gift she gave to me; in turn I have to give her life-long best memory.

He was your best dad who cares your emotions, showed love towards you in this beautiful way. She went to dad and cried.

"No other love in the world is like the love of a father has for his little girl". Father love never ends towards child. He is our real hero.

Not only swecha many children are leaving their passion and goal just to make her parents happy. I hope all the children will get back their dreams as swecha got.